DOG LOVES
FAIRY TALES

LOUISE YATES

RED FOX

In memory of Towser,
who inspired these adventures

Some other books by Louise Yates

A Small Surprise

Frank & Teddy Make Friends

Dog Loves Books

Dog Loves Drawing

Dog Loves Counting

Toad and I

DOG LOVES FAIRY TALES
A RED FOX BOOK 978 1 782 95593 1

First published in Great Britain by Jonathan Cape,
an imprint of Random House Children's Publishers UK
A Penguin Random House Company

Penguin
Random House
UK

Joanthan Cape edition published 2014
Red Fox edition published 2015

1 3 5 7 9 10 8 6 4 2

Copyright © Louise Yates, 2014

The right of Louise Yates to be identified as the author and illustrator of this work has been asserted
in accordance with the Copyright, Designs and Patents Act 1988.

Penguin Random House is committed to a sustainable future for our business, our readers
and our planet. This book is made from Forest Stewardship Council® certified paper.

FSC
www.fsc.org
MIX
Paper from
responsible sources
FSC® C018179

Red Fox Books are published by Random House Children's Publishers UK
61–63 Uxbridge Road, London W5 5SA

www.randomhousechildrens.co.uk
www.randomhouse.co.uk

Addresses for companies within The Random House Group Limited can be found at: www.randomhouse.co.uk/offices.htm

THE RANDOM HOUSE GROUP Limited Reg. No. 954009

A CIP catalogue record for this book is available from the British Library.

Printed in China

Once upon a time, not very long ago,
Dog was dusting his bookshelves when he
found a book that had been buried and lost.

"What luck!" thought Dog, as he dusted it
down and read: *Fairy Tales from Long Ago*.
He opened it up and his adventure began.

The first thing Dog
found was an imp in
a jam jar. Dog lifted
off the lid.

"Put it back on tight!" cried the imp.

"I'm bad luck, I am – I'm
riddled with it! I broke
a witch's wand and she
cursed me and said
I should stay in here
until my luck changed.
It never has."

"Then we must break the curse," said Dog.

He took the imp by his bad-luck hand
and led him out into the Enchanted Forest.

"First," said Dog, "we must find the witch."

"Bad luck," said the imp. "I can't remember where she lives."

"Well, let's try," said Dog. "Don't worry – fairy tales often have happy endings."

"Not for me, they don't," said the imp.

They walked a long way before dusk fell.
"Bad luck," said the imp. "It's getting dark
and we've still not found the witch."
In the darkness, a light began to glow.

Dog knocked on
the window.

"Oh dear," said
the imp, "there's
no one in."

He leaned miserably
against the door and
it creaked open.

Inside, they found
a broken chair,

some cold porridge

and a little girl
asleep in bed.

"Let's ask her where the witch lives," whispered Dog.

"Bad luck!" cried the imp,
forgetting to whisper. "She's asleep!"
And with that, the little girl woke up.

"No!" she said crossly –
she did not know where the witch lived.
"I'm sorry to have woken you," said the imp,
and he and Dog hurried back outside.

There they met three bears
walking up the path:
a daddy bear,
a mummy bear
and a baby bear.

"A very good evening
to you!" called the imp.
The bears waved
back happily.

But when the bears reached the cottage, there came a terrible cry, and Dog and the imp watched as the little girl fled into the forest.

"Oh no!" wailed the imp. "I should never have said a word – I bring everybody bad luck!"

"Don't worry," said Dog, "we'll soon find the witch." "I wish that were true," the imp sighed sadly.

Dog and the imp carried on through the night until
they were too tired to walk any further.

In the morning they were woken by the sound of
grunting, chopping and banging.

They found three little pigs.

Each was building himself a house.

Ah-ah-ah...

Dog and the imp offered to help,

but the straw tickled the imp's nose . . .

Choooo!

. . . which was unfortunate.

"I'm sorry," sniffed the imp. "Bad luck."

The three little pigs decided to move into
the brick house together.

And not even the strongest wind
could blow that house down.

Dog and the imp
went on their way.

"I don't think we'll ever find the witch," said the imp.
"Everything I touch turns bad. I only have to
look at something and it goes wrong."

So he shut his eyes tightly, but then . . .

. . . bumped straight
into a branch.

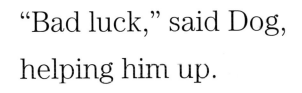

"Bad luck," said Dog,
helping him up.

A little girl joined them further down the path.
She was on her way to her grandmother's house.

When Dog explained who they were looking for,
the little girl pointed them in the direction of a castle.
"Maybe you can see where the witch lives
from the top?" she suggested.

But the imp couldn't
fly that high.
  "Rapunzel! Rapunzel!
Let down your hair!"
he shouted up instead.
There was no answer.
"Bad luck," said the imp.
"She's not here – we'll
have to take the stairs."

But when they got to the top,
they couldn't see out of the window.
There was just a spinning wheel
and more straw.

"Bad luck!" sneezed the imp.

The door flew open . . .

"Ha ha! I've got you!" screeched a little man. The imp took one look at him and fainted. "I'm going to keep you here until you've spun all this straw into gold!"

"But we must find the witch who cursed my friend," said Dog.

"Get spinning," screeched the man, "and if you can guess my name I'll tell you where the witch lives." He slammed the door.

Dog loved spinning! But he hadn't made any gold. "Oh, I have such terrible luck!" cried the imp, when he woke up.

"Who else would run into Rumpelstiltskin twice in three hundred years?"

"You've met him before?" asked Dog.

"Oh yes," he said sadly.

Dog hugged the imp happily. "Rumpelstiltskin!" he called.

The little man seemed very disappointed when he realized that they knew his name.

"The witch lives next door," he grumbled.
"Bad luck," said the imp kindly, as they left.

Next door, they knocked and waited nervously for the witch to answer. But she was delighted to see them!

"My little imp!" she cried. "There you are. Where have you been? I have been looking for you everywhere!"

"You told me to stay in the jam jar until my luck changed and it never did!" said the imp. "Oh, please tell me how to break the curse."

The witch shook her head sadly. "There never was a curse: if you believe you'll always have bad luck, then you're bound to feel stuck. But who gave you hope and helped you out?"

"My friend, Dog," said the imp.

"Then don't you see, little imp? How lucky you are to have found such a good friend!"

Dog and the imp were overjoyed! They did indeed feel fortunate to have found each other. So they continued on together all the way to . . .

And what a
happy ending
it was!

Dog Loves Fairy Tales!

And as Dog closed the book, he knew
that they would live happily ever after.